WITHDRAWN

CHILDRENS Dora
Dora
Beverly Hills Pub   ary

D1505872

I Like to Read® Books
You will like all of them!

Paperback and Hardcover
Boy, Bird, and Dog by David McPhail

Dinosaurs Don't, Dinosaurs Do by Steve Björkman

The Lion and the Mice
by Rebecca Emberley and Ed Emberley

See Me Run by Paul Meisel
A Theodor Seuss Geisel Award Honor Book

Hardcover
Car Goes Far by Michael Garland

Fish Had a Wish by Michael Garland

The Fly Flew In by David Catrow

I Have a Garden by Bob Barner

I Will Try by Marilyn Janovitz

Late Nate in a Race by Emily Arnold McCully

Look! by Ted Lewin

Mice on Ice
by Rebecca Emberley and Ed Emberley

Pig Has a Plan by Ethan Long

Sam and the Big Kids by Emily Arnold McCully

See Me Dig by Paul Meisel

Sick Day by David McPhail

You Can Do It! by Betsy Lewin

Visit holidayhouse.com to read more
about I Like to Read® Books.

J
READER
Garland

Car Goes Far

by Michael Garland

I Like to Read®

Holiday House / New

709.2 MOORE
Moore, Henry, 1898-1986
Henry Moore : sculture,
disegni, grafica
WITHDRAWN
Beverly Hills Public Library

To my son Kevin

I LIKE TO READ is a registered trademark of Holiday House, Inc.

Copyright © 2013 by Michael Garland
All Rights Reserved
HOLIDAY HOUSE is registered in the U.S. Patent and Trademark Office.
Printed and Bound in October 2012 at Tien Wah Press, Johor Bahru, Johor, Malaysia.
The text typeface is Report School.
The artwork was created with mixed digital tools.
www.holidayhouse.com
First Edition
1 3 5 7 9 10 8 6 4 2

Library of Congress Cataloging-in-Publication Data
Garland, Michael, 1952-
Car goes far / by Michael Garland. — 1st ed.
p. cm. — (I like to read)
Summary: After an adventure, a shiny, clean car is in desperate need of a wash.
ISBN 978-0-8234-2598-3 (hardcover)
[1. Automobiles—Fiction. 2. Car washes—Fiction.] I. Title.
PZ7.G18413Car 2013
[E]—dc23
2011049242

Car looks good.

Car goes.

Car goes far.

Oh, no! Smoke gets on Car.

Oh, no!
Birds make a mess on Car.

Car does not look good now.
Car is sad.

Car must wash.

Car gets wet.
Splash, splash.

Car gets suds.

Car gets a rub.
Mmmmmmm.

Car gets wet again.

Car gets dry.

Car looks good again!

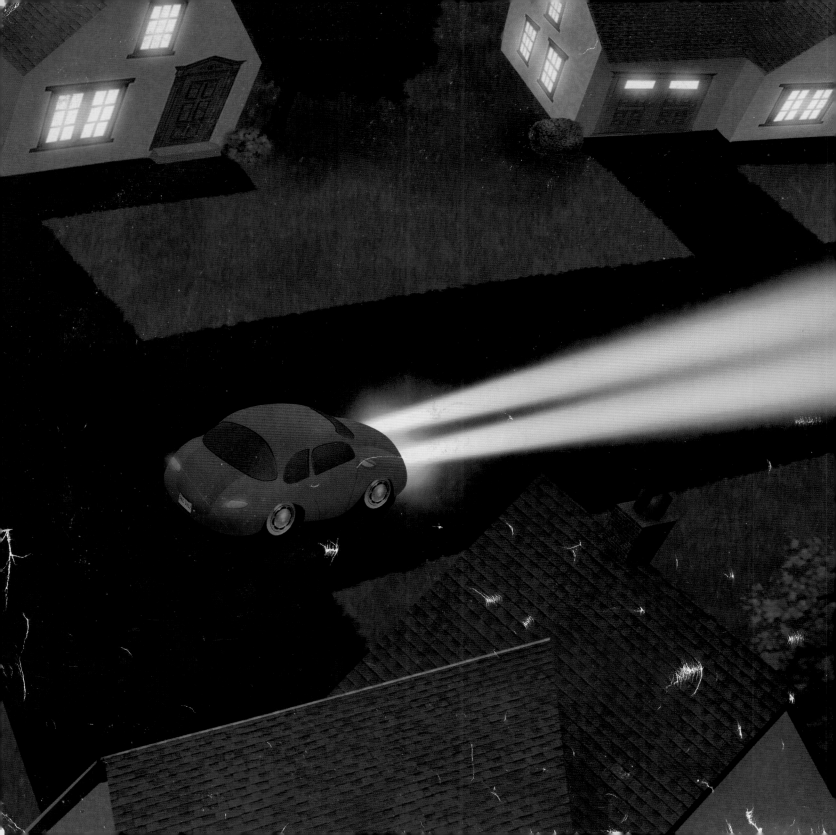